THE EVIL MUMMIES

Colour Work: G. VLOEBERGHS

BY DE GIETER.

9th CINEBOOK
The 9th Art Publisher

Original title: Papyrus – Les momies maléfiques

Original edition: © Dupuis, 1996 by De Gieter
www.dupuis.com
All rights reserved

English translation: © 2010 Cinebook Ltd

Translator: Luke Spear
Lettering and text layout: Imadjinn sarl
Printed in Spain by Just Colour Graphic

This edition first published in Great Britain in 2010 by
Cinebook Ltd
56 Beech Avenue
Canterbury, Kent
CT4 7TA
www.cinebook.com

A CIP catalogue record for this book
is available from the British Library

ISBN 978-1-84918-027-6

Phew!... By Horus, it's so hot!

Aaah! When I think how cool the scented gardens in Thebes are at sunset. The soft murmurs of the Nile under the voluptuous caress of the evening breeze!...

WHAT HAVE I COME TO DO IN THIS HELLHOLE?

Papyrus! You have the honour of taking part in a mission of the utmost importance and you won't stop complaining!

Taking the mummies of 10 archers, Pharaoh Sekenenre's companions, from the Hammamat mines? Pah!

What? Sekenenre-Taa, Pharaoh of the 17th Dynasty, died with 10 of his companions to save Egypt from the Hyksos*. He's the husband of my ancestor, Queen Theti-Tasheri!
It's thanks to their sacrifices that Egypt is free and powerful today! It's thanks to them that you...

All right! All right! Ok!... Still...

*They reigned over Northern Egypt for a century.

We've been crawling through this stifling heat for three days!

Follow Puin's example!

He carries out his role as the donkey chief without a grumble!

Hehe!

Are you still sure of the way, Menenseth?

There's the border marker, Lord Ornes. Here begins the domain of the god Seth, master of the desert.

Fatigue? Negligence? Ignorance? Nobody stopped to pay homage to the terrible god, and a little later...

I suggest we stop here, Princess, and set up camp. Night will soon fall.

All right.

Suits me!

2

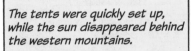
The tents were quickly set up, while the sun disappeared behind the western mountains.

Has anyone seen Khamelot? He's got my pillow!

Oh, look!

Wow, did you see that, Puin? That cloud looks just like your donkey!

Hee-haw!

Wow!

Hohoho!

Hahaha!

That's so funny!

Hohoho!

Stop, fools! You're insulting god Seth's apparition!* You'll provoke his wrath!

What do you think, Papyrus?

Bah! The image is already gone. It's a storm behind the mountain. It won't stop me sleeping.

Her Highness's tent is up! Would you care to do us the honour of spending the night within?

Very good, loyal Papyrus!

*God of the desert

As your vigilant guardian, I will spend the night in front of your door!

After a frugal meal, the strange cloud was forgotten and everyone found somewhere to sleep...

Good night, Papyrus!

or to keep watch.

At the base of the wadi, the night's silence replaced the storm's rumbling.

And Papyrus slept under...

BRRRRRR

the symbol of Amun.

RRRR

BRRRR

!

RRRRRR

I can't sleep with that snoring!

RRRRRRR

Papyrus, what's going on?

What? You're not the one who's... who's...?

4

BRRRRRR

And suddenly, there was terror.

RRR RRRr

From the end of the wadi, a gigantic wave rolled out, sweeping up everything in its way.

PAPYRUS, HELP!

Quick! Hold on to the...

Papyrus, look out!

Heee-haw!

Later...

WAAAH!

By Horus! What am I doing here?

Oh, I remember! The camp... Seth's black cloud... The deluge that swept up everything... I was thrown onto the rocks!...

Alone!... All the others have perished!... No water... no supplies...

I'm going to die a slow death!

Oh! Close my eyes... lean forward and... end it all now!...

?

My magic sword!

I have to grab it from the falcon's clutches!

Oh, no!

The magic sword pierced the ground at the bottom of the rocks with a flash...

Tok

Tok

Tok

TCHAK

And, suddenly, fire lit up the desert, leaving an arrow of fire!

7

It's a sign! By Horus! My sword is showing me the way!

In that immense desert, without the slightest bit of shade, the heat very soon became scorching.

Hours passed. The march became an ordeal.

Aagh! My feet are burning!

I thought I was stronger than I am... I won't make it any further. I... I...

Half-unconscious, Papyrus woke with a start. Under his fingers, he felt a metallic object...

What's this...?

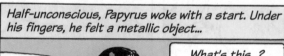

Theti-Cheri's bracelet? That's impossible!...

She came this way!

I must... get up... carry on... I... have... to... find... her!

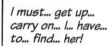

Papyrus stood and began walking... for another hour.

When suddenly...

The falcon?

Oh, no!

What a trick! That bird of sorrow must have brought the jewel out here... Theti is far away... maybe dead!

DE GIETER.

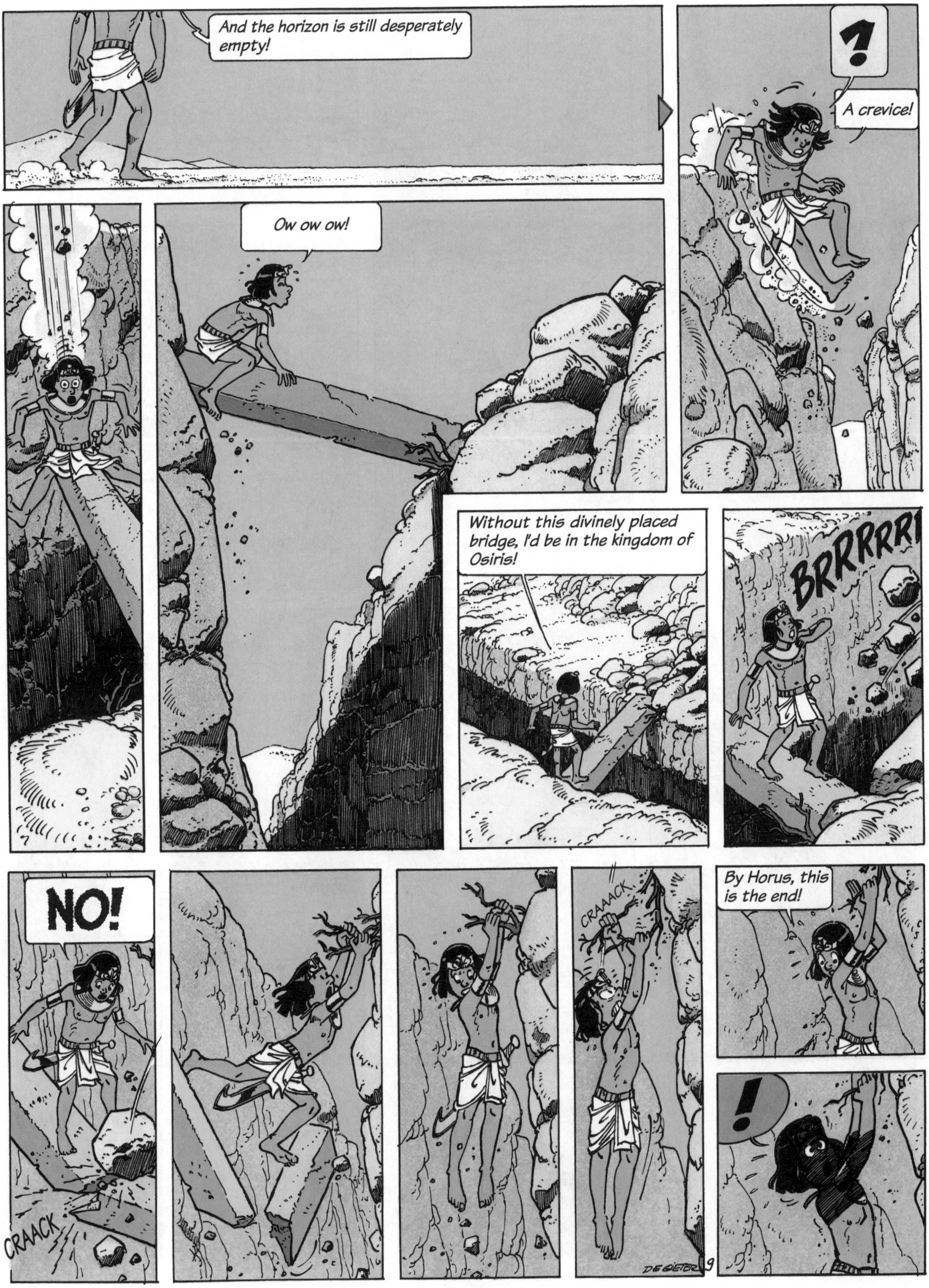
And the horizon is still desperately empty!
?
A crevice!
Ow ow ow!
Without this divinely placed bridge, I'd be in the kingdom of Osiris!
BRRRRR
NO!
CRAACK
CRAACK
By Horus, this is the end!
!
DE GIETER

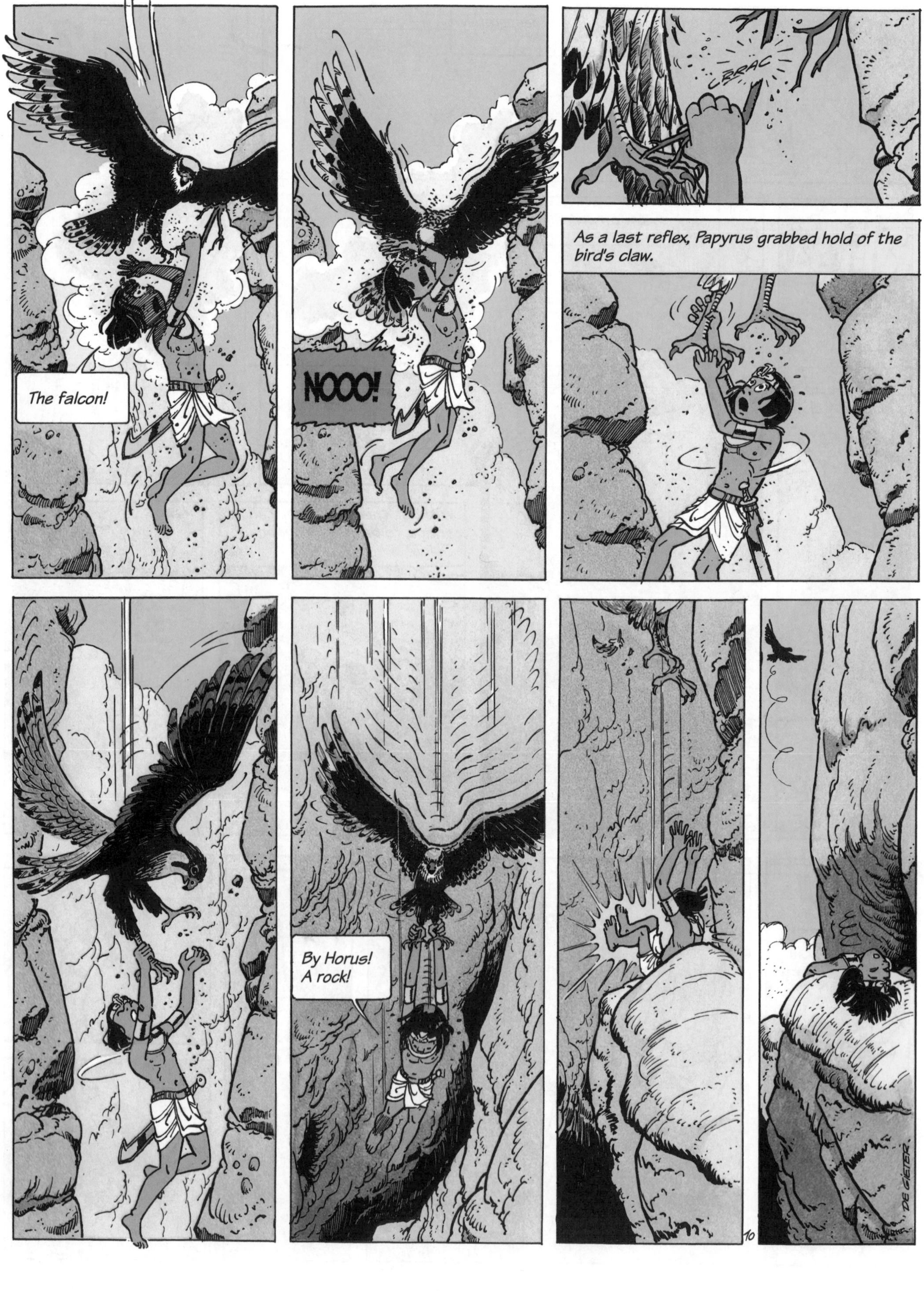

The falcon!
NOOO!
C-BRAC
As a last reflex, Papyrus grabbed hold of the bird's claw.
By Horus! A rock!
DE GIETER

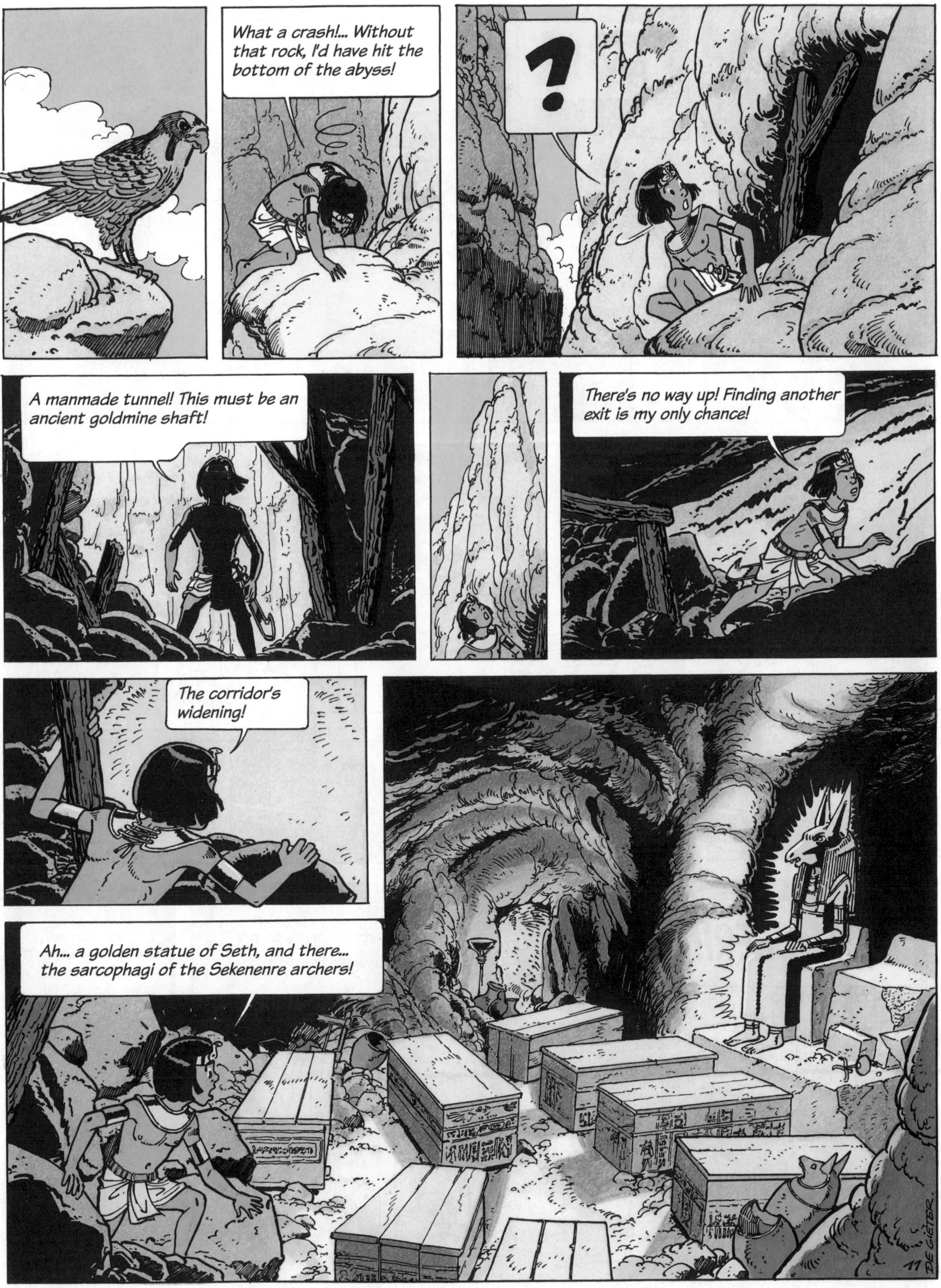
What a crash!... Without that rock, I'd have hit the bottom of the abyss!
?
A manmade tunnel! This must be an ancient goldmine shaft!
There's no way up! Finding another exit is my only chance!
The corridor's widening!
Ah... a golden statue of Seth, and there... the sarcophagi of the Sekenenre archers!
DE GIETER
11

AAGH!

I'm sure of it now! Those are the Sekenenre archer mummies!

I'd rather not hang around here. Where's the way out?

?

MNMMM

An... an open sarc... ophagus!

NMMNM

Brave...

But not foolhardy!

MNMMN

NO!

THETI-CHERI!

MNMNMM

By all the gods! What are you doing in there?

Papyrus, protect me!

I'm scared! I'm scared!

Come on; calm down, Theti!

12

SETH'S CURSE IS UPON US!...

THE MUMMIES ARE ALIVE!

Alive? That's not possible!

SHRIEEEKKK

LOOK OUT!

SHRIEEEK

TCHAAK

A golden arrow?... If I hadn't dived!

Quick! There's a way out. Let's get out of here!

But Theti-Cheri stayed, petrified.

Looming out of the shadows, an unspeakable being advanced, blocking the passage.

Theti, save yourself!

13

Living mummies! I never thought they could exist! We have to get out now!

Theti, where are you?

RAAAW

By Horus! I'll have to get rid of this bandaged fright first!

But the "fright" didn't wait for an attack...

CRACK

... Papyrus instinctively raised his sword in front of himself.

TCHAAK

RRAAF AAW

By all the gods! The vault's giving way... It's all going to fall!

BRRRROOOMM

By Horus! He wasn't as lucky as I was!

PAPYRUS, HELP HELP

That sounds like...

Theti! I'm coming!

HELP

Suddenly emerging from the tunnel, Papyrus teetered, blinded by the dazzling sun, and...

AAAAAGH!

SPLASH!

The mine's well?

DE GIETER.

15

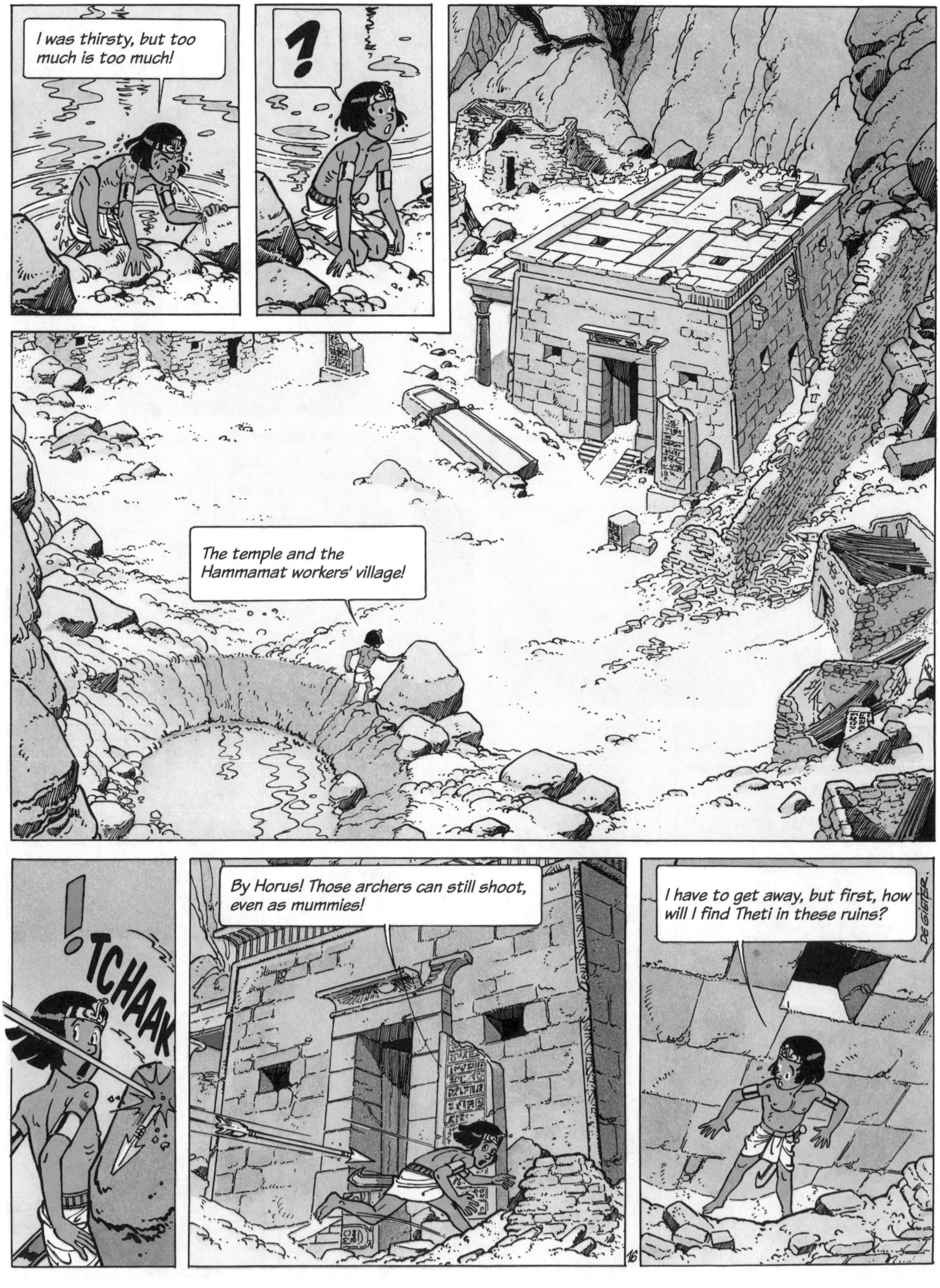
I was thirsty, but too much is too much!
!
The temple and the Hammamat workers' village!
!
TCHAAK
By Horus! Those archers can still shoot, even as mummies!
I have to get away, but first, how will I find Theti in these ruins?
DE GIETER
16

BLOOD?

BY ALL THE GODS! THETI IS ON THE ROOF, INJURED!

Another Seth statue!

THETI?

Theti... are you alive? Are you hurt? What happened?

Oh, Papyrus!

The... the mummy... took me to offer me to the god Seth. I escaped to the roof. It followed me, and the falcon attacked it; it backed off... and fell down the stairs!

SHRIEEEEK

The god Horus himself saved me!

He warned me with his blood!

We're at the mercy of the god Seth, but Horus is protecting us!

He may be, but we can't stay here. Come on!

The mummy disappeared!

RRHAAAAW!

WAAAH!

THETI, SAVE YOURSELF! THEY'RE INVINCIBLE!

AAAAAGH!

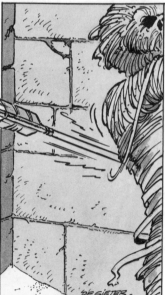

18

DE GIETER.

20

Even my magic sword didn't make him back up!

Only golden arrows forged by Seth can defeat one of Seth's creatures!

It's awful!

No! Like the other mummy, it has found peace again!

Let's hope there were no more!

Meanwhile, in the archers' crypt...

We have to get out of this ghost village now!

You're right, but how? We're victims of Seth's wrath...

... prisoners in this basin. There's no way out save the mine shafts. But which one will take us to freedom?

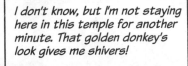

I don't know, but I'm not staying here in this temple for another minute. That golden donkey's look gives me shivers!

AAAAGH!

BAM

But, Papyrus, what's going on?

The... mummies! Two more have turned up!

Luckily, the door is solid and the first one through will...

NO! THEY... THEY... THERE!

PAPYRUS!

Don't move—I'm coming!

Hurry up!

AAAGH!

What now?

The door, now! Let's get out of here!

By all the gods! It... it... won't open!

Papyrus, look out!

CRACK!

Now's our chance!

The other mummy!? Too late!

BOOM!

By Horus! That was some collision!

This time they won't get in our way!

No! There are two more!

Already?

Turn around! Quick! The other way out!

OUCH!

OW!

???

Papyrus?... Are you OK?...

I'll be better when you gedd your foodd off by face!

We can't hang around. We have to find another way out!

Look! There's another corridor!

By Horus! Let's go this way!

Quick! I can hear them! They're on our heels!

By Anubis! It's a dead end!

Papyrus, they're coming!

Papyrus! What are you doing?

Look out! Get back!

Look at the mummies! Those two don't like water!

But, Papyrus, we'll be drowned too!

Don't panic! Take a deep breath and follow me!

Horus! Don't let him be crazy!

So, is that better? Hahaha!

Where are we?

In the mine's well!

But how did you know...?

Ha!... I started the mine visit this way, and that tunnel was only abandoned because it led to the well. When pierced, the well emptied out in an instant!

But Theti had already stopped listening to his explanations.

Papyrus, look!

Golden Horus statues?

The receding water freed them!

That's why everything's hostile towards us here. Horus, the protector, has been defeated by Seth, who reigns alone over the desert. He's the one who invokes the cursed forces and uses mummies to destroy us!

That's awful!

SHRIIIIEK!

PAPYRUS, LOOK OUT!

SHRIIIEK!

Two more mummies!

Will it never end!

Quick! Do this!

You think that...?

Faced with the two Horuses, the mummies hesitated...

backed off and then ran.

Victory! We're rid of those walking bandages!

Hey, Papyrus! Don't celebrate too early; tell me how to get out of here! The corridor is flooded and the well walls are too slippery!

After much thought...

I'VE GOT IT!

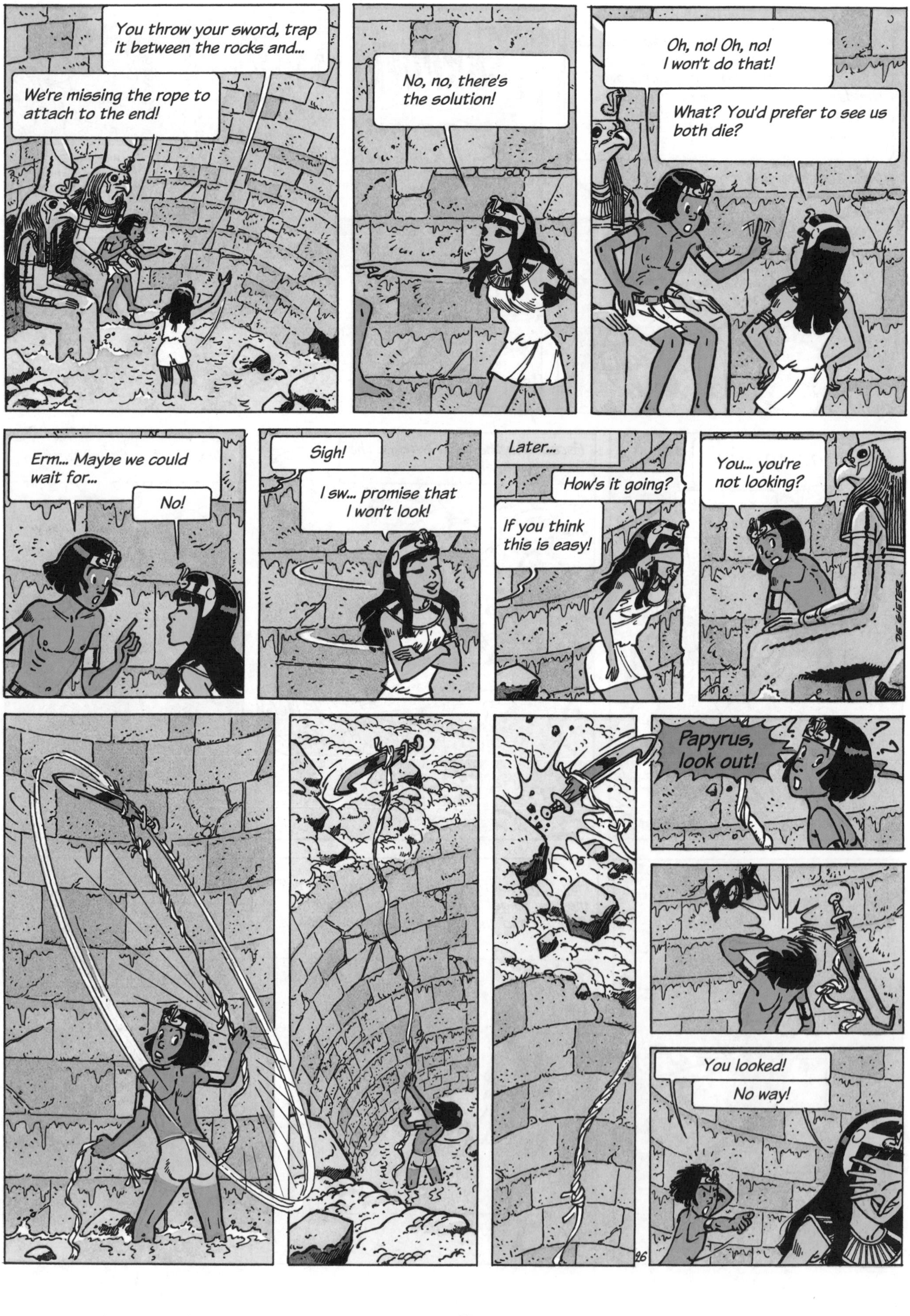

We're missing the rope to attach to the end!
You throw your sword, trap it between the rocks and...
No, no, there's the solution!
Oh, no! Oh, no! I won't do that!
What? You'd prefer to see us both die?
Erm... Maybe we could wait for...
No!
Sigh!
I sw... promise that I won't look!
Later...
How's it going?
If you think this is easy!
You... you're not looking?
Papyrus, look out!
POK
You looked!
No way!

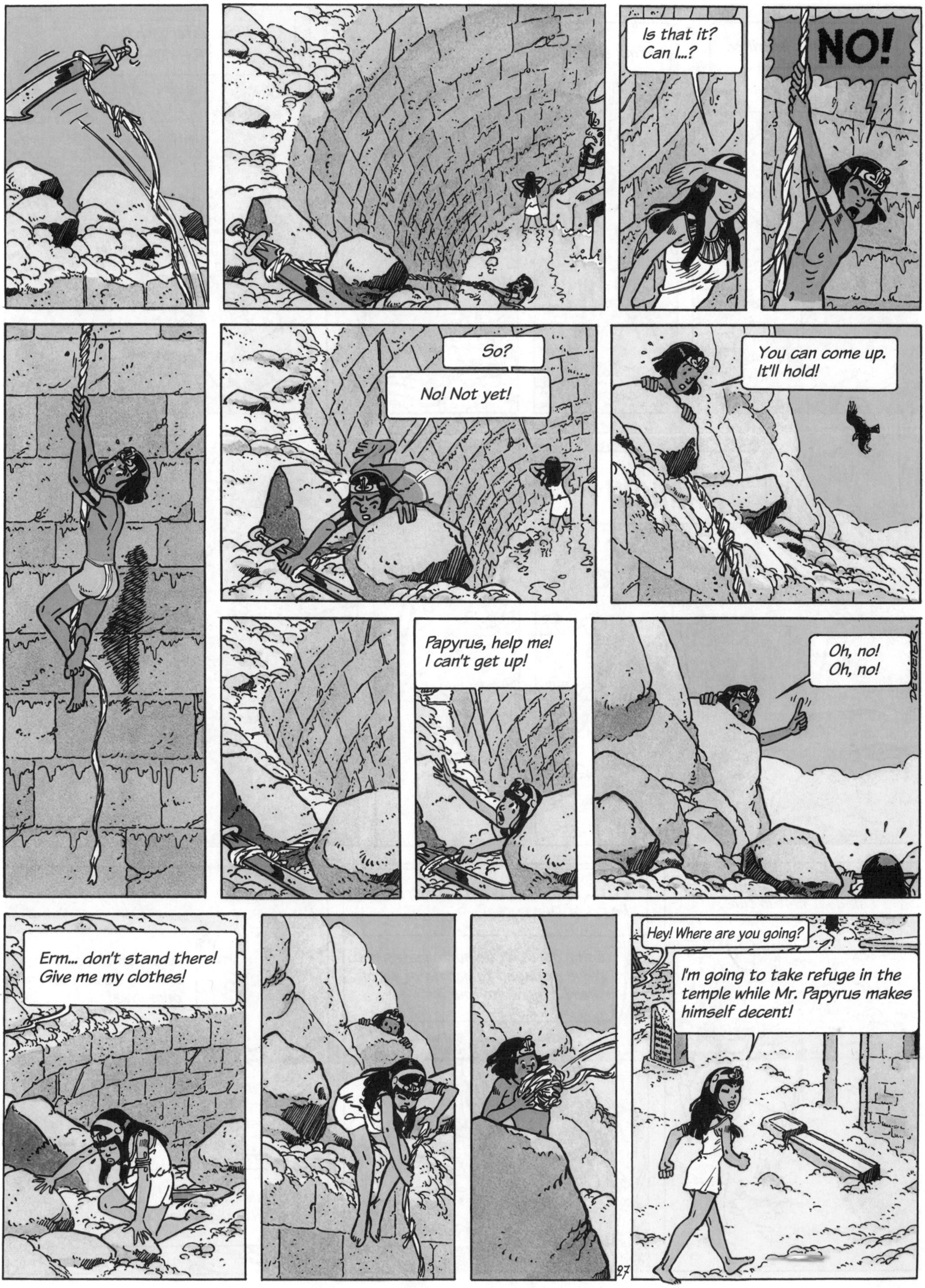
Is that it? Can I...?
NO!
So?
No! Not yet!
You can come up. It'll hold!
Papyrus, help me! I can't get up!
Oh, no! Oh, no!
Erm... don't stand there! Give me my clothes!
Hey! Where are you going?
I'm going to take refuge in the temple while Mr. Papyrus makes himself decent!

Mmmblmm... sacrifice yourself... and as thanks...

Erm... there!

My sword!

I feel safer with it! Are you there, Theti?

RHAAAAA

What the...? **AAAAGH!**

TCHAK

I made it just in time, once again!

Pfft!... By Horus! When will we be rid of this curse?

Come on! Don't be such a pessimist. We've managed to get rid of six of them!... There are four left!

And with the golden arrows, we can defend ourselves!

Shhh!... Not so loud. Seth might hear us!

I still feel like he's watching us!

Don't be such a pessimist!

I'm not a pessimist. I'm tired! Can you believe what we've been through since last night?

We have to get out of this hellhole before Seth invents other horrors!

Bah! For now, it's all right!...

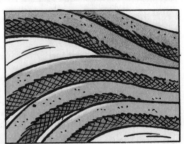

PAPYRUS!

Hm?

EEEEEEEEE

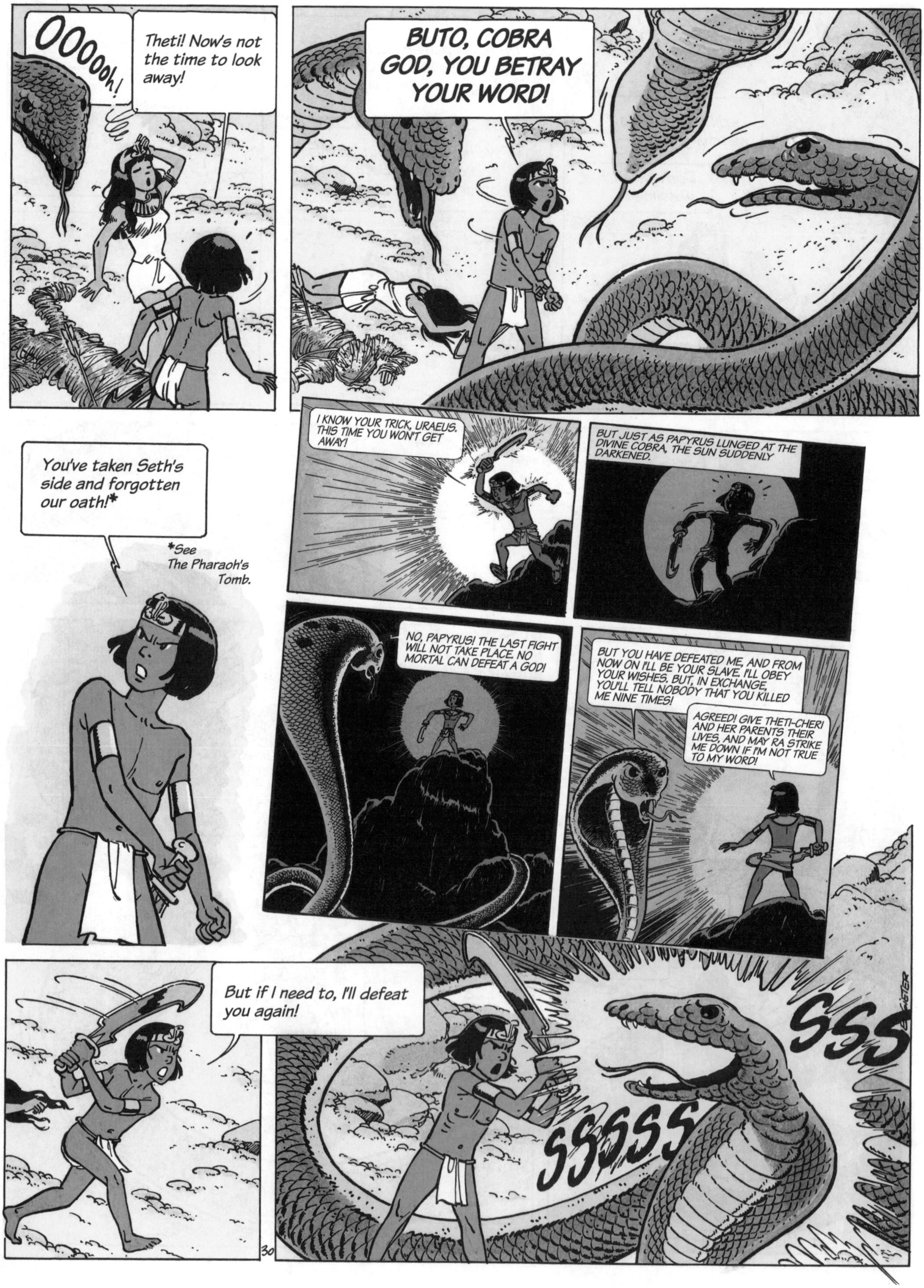

OOOOoh!
Theti! Now's not the time to look away!
BUTO, COBRA GOD, YOU BETRAY YOUR WORD!
You've taken Seth's side and forgotten our oath!*
*See The Pharaoh's Tomb.
I KNOW YOUR TRICK, URAEUS. THIS TIME YOU WON'T GET AWAY!
BUT JUST AS PAPYRUS LUNGED AT THE DIVINE COBRA, THE SUN SUDDENLY DARKENED.
NO, PAPYRUS! THE LAST FIGHT WILL NOT TAKE PLACE. NO MORTAL CAN DEFEAT A GOD!
BUT YOU HAVE DEFEATED ME, AND FROM NOW ON I'LL BE YOUR SLAVE. I'LL OBEY YOUR WISHES. BUT, IN EXCHANGE, YOU'LL TELL NOBODY THAT YOU KILLED ME NINE TIMES!
AGREED! GIVE THETI-CHERI AND HER PARENTS THEIR LIVES, AND MAY RA STRIKE ME DOWN IF I'M NOT TRUE TO MY WORD!
But if I need to, I'll defeat you again!
SSSSS
SSS
30

Wow!?

Another one of Seth's evil tricks!

Those cobras never existed!

Oh! Theti fainted! Poor thing!

Oh, no, she's asleep! Hey, Theti!

No point waking her, but we should take shelter!

There! If Seth's bandaged henchmen turn up, I can give them a good welcome! Hehe!

And from here, I can see the whole area. I'll keep watch while Theti sleeps...

... and clever be the one who takes me... by surprise... ZZZ!

31

But someone else was watching from on high.

SHRIEEEK!!

Mu... mummies!

By Horus! My weapons! My sword! They're still behind the wall!

AAAGH! Too much! It's too much!

It's the last four!

... And they're more horrid than the others!

There! A tunnel! I'm saved!

NO!

DE GIETER.

34

Will you let go!?

!

By Horus! This time I'm done for!

Well... what's got into them?

I'll be a mummy if I understand any of it!

HEE HAW!

Khamelot, it was you?

That's great! You made it just in time! You escaped from the tidal wave too, and you found us!...

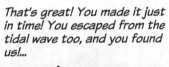

... And with your great big ears, the mummies took you for an apparition of the god Seth!

Hee haw!

33

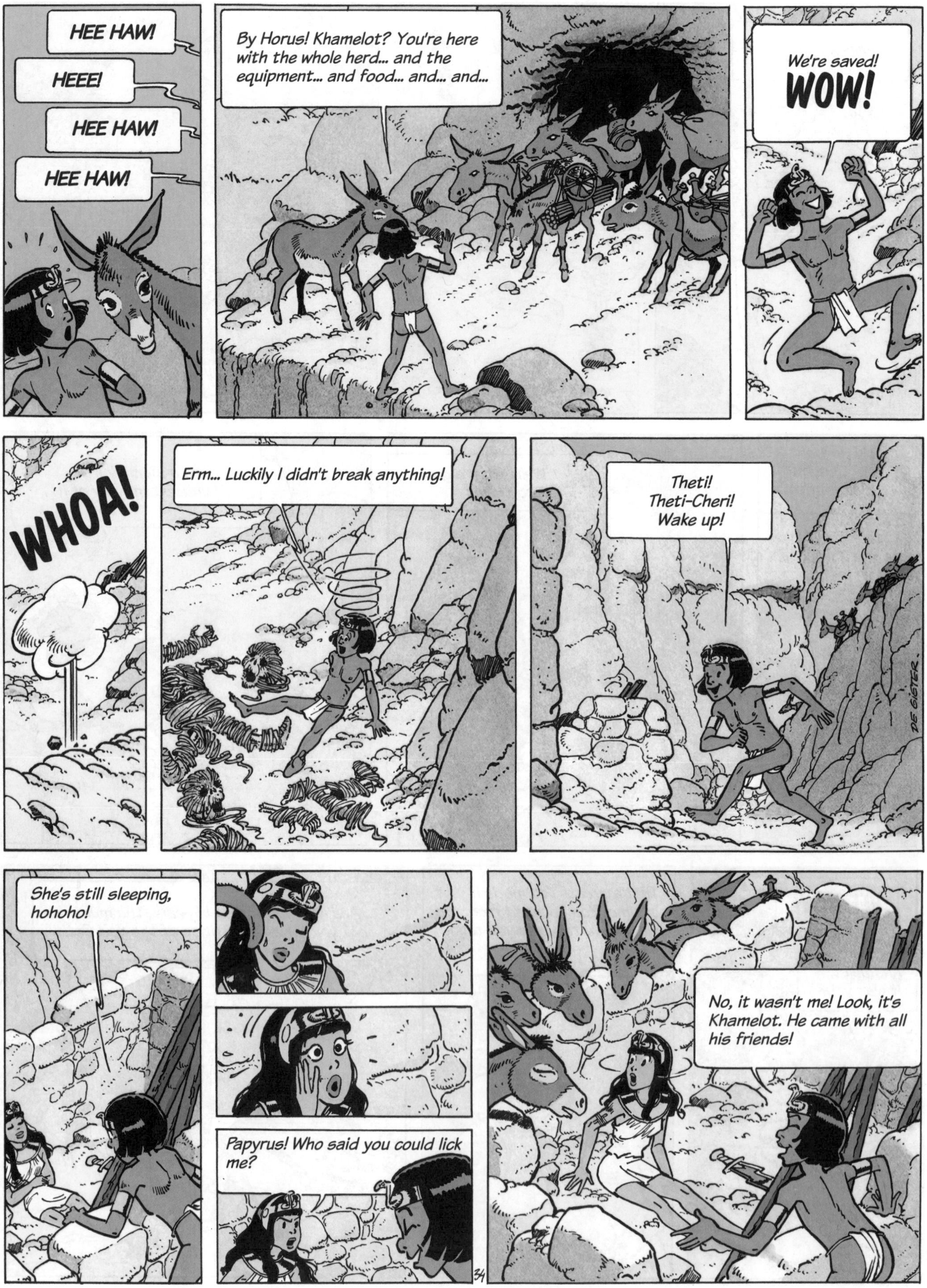
HEE HAW!
HEEE!
HEE HAW!
HEE HAW!
By Horus! Khamelot? You're here with the whole herd... and the equipment... and food... and... and...
We're saved!
WOW!
WHOA!
Erm... Luckily I didn't break anything!
Theti! Theti-Cheri! Wake up!
DE GIETER
She's still sleeping, hohoho!
Papyrus! Who said you could lick me?
34
No, it wasn't me! Look, it's Khamelot. He came with all his friends!

They're here with water, food, clothes...

Clothes?

Wait!

I'll be back!

Hehe! I did well to remember a spare loincloth for the trip!

The latest fashion from Thebes!

... Just my sword and we can go!

Wait! I had a dream. Horus appeared to me. He asked us to restore the balance of Maat in the valley!... We have to put the golden statues back in place!

Meaning?

You can pull!

Gently... good... a little more...

HEE HAW!

Go, Khamelot!

Later...

There, side by side once again, the protector of Egypt and the desert god!

Night fell when the second Horus statue was put in place.

Lucky that poor Puin hadn't unloaded all his donkeys. But without a royal tent, you'll have to sleep under the beautiful stars, Princess!

WHACK WHACK
CLACK
WHACK
CLACK

The next day...

Aaah! What a good night! I slept wonderfully!

... And you, Pa...
AAAGH!

Me, too, apart from the mosquitoes!

35

I won't stay a minute longer in this hellhole! The donkeys have found the exit—let's go!

Wait! We still have something to do!...

Horus appeared to me last night!

AGAIN!

He reminded me of our mission: to take the archers' mummies to Thebes!

What? You want to take those... those bone packages with us?... Those monsters who nearly killed us? Never!

We're taking them! I give the orders here!

OK, OK! All right! All right!

Grrmblmm ✦◎❋✊ mmmble grmmbl...

Papyrus! Stop grumbling. We came to get these mummies. Horus has ordered me to, and we're taking them back!

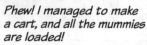

Phew! I managed to make a cart, and all the mummies are loaded!

The "whole ones" on the donkeys!...

36

And the erm... pieces on the cart!

PAPYRUS, LOOK OUT!

By Horus!... Maybe I didn't quite balance out the load!

HEE HAW!

After a few... adjustments, the caravan left the cursed mine.

An adventure that's finally over! In a few days we'll be back home. Ahhh!... Back to Thebes...

By Horus! There he goes again!

... Back to the coolness of the scented gardens. The soft murmur of the Nile under the voluptuous caress of the evening breeze!...

Papyrus, stop!

PAPYRUS, STOP!

My papyrus!

By all the gods! What's he doing in the middle of the desert?

His stick shows he's a royal prospector*. He's crossing the desert looking for new copper, gold or stone veins!...

*A geologist

There's your papyrus. Don't be upset—there's nothing written on it!

Give me my papyrus! It's mine!

Of course, m'lady. If I write down my notes, others will steal my discoveries!

37

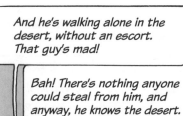

And he's walking alone in the desert, without an escort. That guy's mad!

Bah! There's nothing anyone could steal from him, and anyway, he knows the desert. He has nothing to fear!...

ROGUE! SCOUNDREL! THIEF!

... Except meeting another prospector!

USELESS!

WORTHLESS PROSPECTOR!

OUT OF MY SIGHT!

YOU NEVER KNEW THE DIFFERENCE BETWEEN A GOLD AND A SILVER VEIN!

BETWEEN FELDSPAR AND CARNALLITE

JADE AND MANGANESE!

TURQUOISE AND GALENA!

And the journey continued...

Four days of dragging these mummies under a heavy sun, and we're still in Seth's domain. Grmmm... we're barely moving!

It's our divine mission. Until now we've avoided pillagers; that's the main thing!

Pah! Our load will hardly make them drool!

PAPYRUS, LOOK!

We spoke too soon!

We're done for!

Maybe they didn't see us. There, rocks! Let's hide!

Just in time!

Shhhh!...

Well... wow!

DE GIETER.

Ostriches!

Desert pillagers? Hahaha! That's hilarious!

WAH!

Hey! Papyrus?

What happened?

BOOM CRA BAM

Hey! Papyrus! Answer me!

Theti, tie up the donkeys! Come down here on a rope!... Bring a torch and something to light it with!...

Look and tell me what you think of that!

39

By Horus!... 10 sarcophagi?... With the Sekenenre-Taa cartouche?

These must certainly be the sarcophagi of the 10 archers that we had to take back to Thebes!

Then... the other 10?

Yeah! The ones you've had us drag around for four days?

Could they be just miners who died in the mine?...

And yet you assured me that Horus came to you in a dream and asked you to take them?

Erm... yes, he must have been mistaken... or maybe I misheard?

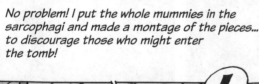

We just have to swap them around!

Right then!

Later...

Phew!

And there's the tomb resealed!

You did put the mummies back in place, Papyrus?

No problem! I put the whole mummies in the sarcophagi and made a montage of the pieces... to discourage those who might enter the tomb!

!

This tomb has not been found since. Egyptologists, be warned!

I hope our problems are over!

We're not far from the paths normally taken by caravans. Guard posts protect them!

YOO! YOO! YOO! YOO! YOO!

!

YOO! YOO! YOO! YOO!

Here we go again! And this time, it's not ostriches!

Who we could have talked to, at least!...

By Horus! I recognise this place!

That won't help us now!

It might!

TCHAK

Once more, the seeping oil caught fire.

41. DE GIETER.

Not bad!
They're scarpering like hares!

But how did you know that the ground would catch fire?

Oh!... Just a little thing that I perfected last time I passed by!

Hey? Where have our donkeys gone?

They've scarpered too!

Stop! Come back! Stop!

... into the abyss of the wadi!

And the ground's sloped too!...

... Straight ahead...

Quiiick! Help me!

It's awful. We're going to...

... to...

?

What are you waiting for?

By Ra! Could it be possible?

Papyrus, don't move. I'll be right back!

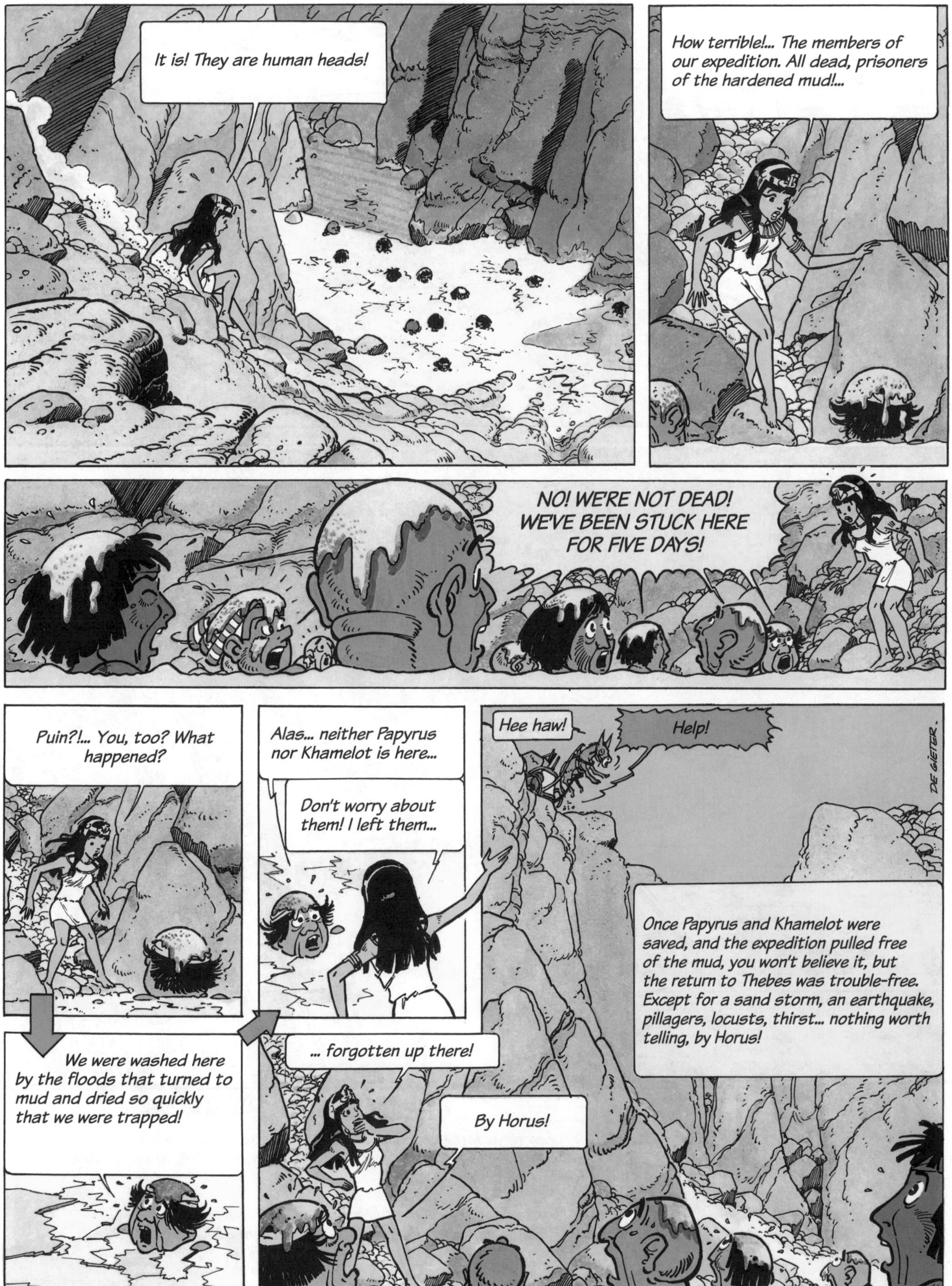

It is! They are human heads!
How terrible!... The members of our expedition. All dead, prisoners of the hardened mud!...
NO! WE'RE NOT DEAD! WE'VE BEEN STUCK HERE FOR FIVE DAYS!
Puin?!... You, too? What happened?
We were washed here by the floods that turned to mud and dried so quickly that we were trapped!
Alas... neither Papyrus nor Khamelot is here...
Don't worry about them! I left them...
... forgotten up there!
By Horus!
Hee haw!
Help!
Once Papyrus and Khamelot were saved, and the expedition pulled free of the mud, you won't believe it, but the return to Thebes was trouble-free. Except for a sand storm, an earthquake, pillagers, locusts, thirst... nothing worth telling, by Horus!
DE GIETER
43

A few days later, with the utmost discretion, the 10 archers of Sekenenre-Taa came to join their 50 fellow archers*, already interred deep within the temple.**

*Died under the reign of Mentuhotep, 11th Dynasty
** That's where archaeologists found them 3000 years later.

THE END

DE GIETER . 96

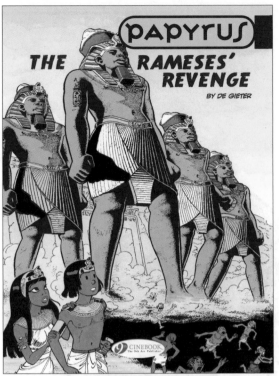

1 - THE RAMESES' REVENGE

2 - IMHOTEP'S TRANSFORMATION

3 - TUTANKHAMUN
THE ASSASSINATED PHARAOH

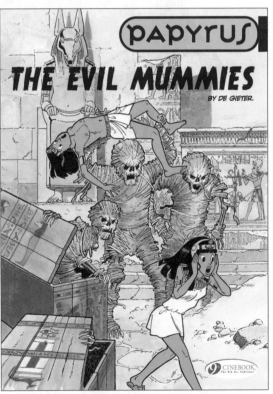

4 - THE EVIL MUMMIES

PAPYRUS

DE GIETER.